Godmama's
House

Johnson

IRENE JENNIE
AND THE CHRISTMAS
MASQUERADE
THE JOHNKANKUS

by Irene Smalls
Illustrated by Melodye Rosales

Little, Brown and Company
Boston   New York   Toronto   London

For my godmother, Louise Godfrey McNeil, who taught me "I Love You, Black Child"
And I would like to thank the Johnkankus for choosing me
— I. S.

Special thanks to Chuck Mercer Photography, Urbana, Illinois;
Nana Lee Raphael-Schirmer, Krannert Costume Department, University of Illinois;
Professor John Perpener III; Reuben Kirksey; Tara Guilamo; Rabiah Haymon;
Andre Mallory; Duane B. Davis; Jermaine Singleton; Harry Warren, Assistant Director,
Cape Fear Museum, Wilmington, North Carolina; Charla Henry; Shanne — Ron —
Shareta and Charlene Miles; Mae Davis; Professor William Berry; Brian Berry;
Jasmine Collins; Chris and Kaye Benson; to my loving family — Giraldo, Dino,
Harmony, and Sinfonia — and to my mom, who is always there for me.
— M. R.

Text copyright © 1996 by Irene Smalls
Illustrations copyright © 1996 by Melodye Rosales

First Edition

Library of Congress Cataloging-in-Publication Data

Smalls, Irene.
    Irene Jennie and the Christmas masquerade : the Johnkankus / by Irene Smalls ; illustrated by Melodye Rosales. — 1st ed.
    p. cm.
    Summary: On a North Carolina plantation, a young slave girl's Christmas is brightened by the Johnkankus parade she witnesses as she waits for her parents to come home.
    ISBN 0-316-79878-9
    [1. Slavery — Fiction. 2. Christmas — Fiction.] I. Rosales, Melodye, ill. II. Title.
PZ7.S63915Is 1996
[E] — dc20   93-7037

10 9 8 7 6 5 4 3 2 1

NIL

Published simultaneously in Canada by Little, Brown & Company (Canada) Limited
and in Great Britain by Little, Brown and Company (UK) Limited

Printed in Italy

Author's Note

African-American slaves were some of the first environmentalists. Out of found objects, recycled materials, garbage, and genius, they made masks, costumes, instruments, and props for a yearly Christmas event, the Johnkankus. In celebrating the Johnkankus, they were continuing an African folkway but also creating one of the first African-American traditions.

The Johnkankus was celebrated by the entire community, both blacks and whites. During the eighteenth and nineteenth centuries along the coast of North Carolina, as well as in many other places in the South, this festival was the most popular musical tradition. On Christmas Day, troupes of as many as a hundred slaves would march through the countryside, singing and dancing.

The Johnkankus is believed to have originated in West Africa and to have been brought first to the West Indies and then to America by the slaves. There evidently was an actual person on the Guinea Coast called John Conny. Some sources refer to a John Connu as a celebrated *cabececera*, or head of a tribe, at Tres Puntas, in Axim, on the Guinea Coast, about the year 1720. The festival was renowned for its unusual costumes and masks and also for the invention of original songs and chants, loudly and rhythmically performed to the accompaniment of bones, cows' horns, drums, and triangles. All the songs in the following story are authentic.

The celebration of the Johnkankus by African Americans died out around 1863, after the end of slavery, when it began to be ridiculed as a low-class slave tradition. White Americans, however, continued the Johnkankus tradition until the early 1900s. In present times, the Gombé dancers perform at festivals in Bermuda, and the John Konny Festival — masks, costumes, instruments, and all — is still celebrated in Jamaica.

Sources

Harriet A. Jacobs. *Incidents in the Life of a Slave Girl, Written by Herself.* Cambridge, Mass.: Harvard University Press, 1987.

Nancy R. Ping. "Black Musical Activities in Antebellum Wilmington, North Carolina." *The Black Perspective in Music* 8 (1980): 139-155.

Richard Walser. "His Worship the John Kuner." *North Carolina Folklore Journal* 19 (1971): 160-172.

In de morning when I rise,
I tell my Jesus howdy.
I wash my hands in de morning glory,
Tell my Jesus howdy.

The Godmother's song and the early morning Carolina sun sparkling in the speckled dew told Irene Jennie that Christmas had arrived. But Irene Jennie didn't feel the Christmas spirit at all.

The Godmother was happy and in full voice. She was one of the best cooks at the big house, and as a reward for her skill, she had been given extra rations as a Christmas gift. After having cooked all day Christmas Eve for the master's Christmas feast, the Godmother was now baking cakes and pies for Christmas Day in the quarters.

"Makes sure you wash behind them ears. Got so much dirt behind 'em you could grow taters," the Godmother jested.

"Yes'm," Irene Jennie whispered. She finished bathing and dressed.

The Godmother continued singing in her low, sweet lullaby voice as she plaited Irene Jennie's hair.

Jesus make the dumb to speak,
Jesus make the cripple walk.
Jesus give the blind his sight,
Jesus do most anything.

Christmas on the plantation was usually a time of jubilee, but on this Christmas Day, Irene Jennie was sad. Her daddy, Charles Hubert, who was known far and wide as a fine fiddlin' man, had been rented out by Massa McNeil to the neighboring plantation for a Christmas party. Mary Ellen, Irene Jennie's mama, had been rented out, too, to help with the cooking for the party. Irene Jennie did not know if they would be back home before Christmas was all over or if they would ever come back at all.

"Godmama," Irene Jennie said, "do you think if'n I asked Massa, he would bring my mama and daddy home?"

"Now, you hush, chile. Don't ask the devil not to sin. You can't ask Massa nothin'. Chile, you don't want to know trouble like that," the Godmother cautioned.

"Buts Godmama, I'se gots no family on Christmas Day. 'Ceptin' you, of course."

The Godmother just shook her head. "Chile, I knows the feel you're feeling."

Irene Jennie studied for a few moments, and then she said with a sigh, "Godmama, does the Lord care 'bout little colored girls?"

"Chile, his eye's on the sparrow. Follow the spirit. The spirit won't lead you far from wrong," the Godmother said.

Irene Jennie closed her eyes and silently prayed with all the spirit she could muster. *Lord, if'n you could see your way clear on this your most special day, Lord, all I wants for Christmas is my mama and daddy back.*

The Godmother came over to Irene Jennie, sitting in the corner of the cabin, and murmured, "Rest your nerves, chile. You won't be cryin' and feeling sad once those Koners git here." She gave Irene Jennie a gentle pat on the head, then turned back to her baking.

Koners. Just hearing the name made Irene Jennie think of smiling. *Koners* was one of the names for the members of the Johnkankus troupe. For as long as Irene Jennie could remember, the Johnkankus had marched through the quarters on Christmas Day, spreading the Christmas spirit, bringing with them a melee of fun and laughter. By any name — Koners, Johnkankus, or John Coners — the troupe of musicians, dancers, and singers meant a great time.

"Godmama, even the funniest parade can't take 'way my sadness today," Irene Jennie whispered.

Suddenly Kevin, the slave quarter lookout, came running up the road breathless with excitement. "The Johnkankus is a-comin'! The Johnkankus is a-comin'!" he shouted at each slave-cabin. Irene Jennie headed for the door. Outside she joined a crowd. It seemed that everyone was rushing toward the roadway.

The Godmother busted out of the door, too, apron flying. "I'se right behind you, chile," she called. Young or old, no one wanted to miss the Johnkankus.

Irene Jennie, peering on tippy-toe at the front edge of the crowd, said, "Godmama, I'se can just see the line of Koners a-marching up the main road." The hard-packed dirt road shook, echoing the arriving presence of the Koners. The soft North Carolina breeze carried the first notes of their song:

Hah, low, here we go,
Hah, low, here we go,
Koners comin'!
Hah, low, here we go,
Koners comin,' cooommin'!

"Koners coming," Irene Jennie sang along. The music of the Koners started coming fast and furious. Jubilantly they marched into the quarter.

First came two acrobats in calico wrappers, wearing long black feathers in their caps. The calico nets that covered their bodies were covered in strips of tattered cloth — yellow, green, blue, red. The strips of brightly colored cloth were haranguing the air, twisting this way then that with the spirited dancing, in frenzied motion to the music.

"Blow dat horn!" the crowd yelled. The Koners had all manner of horns — cow horns, sheep horns, and bull horns — and each musician seemed to play using every breath in his body.

"Ta-ta, ta-ta!" Irene Jennie cupped her hands and made her own Koner horn.

"Blow dat horn!" the crowd yelled again. And blow the horns the ragtag band of Koners did, sharp notes and tatters tearing the sky.

For the longest time, everyone danced wildly, hands in the air. The crowd was singing and shouting. "The Koners are here!" they cried.

Swept up by the rhythms and colors, Irene Jennie bobbed up and down, her arms and legs flailing to the Koner beat. "Godmama, I'se don't know what part of the Johnkankus I likes best," she said, "the dancers, the acrobats, the singers, or them musicians."

On and on into the afternoon, the Koners came down the road, up toward the big house. Some wore horns; some wore old caps. Billowing gossamer clouds of cloth sprang from their shoulders. They blew horns, beat drums, and danced funny birdy steps, mincing and prancing as they came.

Christmas comes but once a year,
Ho rang du rango,
Let everybody have a share,
Ho rang du rango.

"And the children is the honey pods, juba, juba," Irene Jennie and all the children laughingly answered.

"Ho rang du rango. Juba! Juba o, ye juba!" called the singers.

"Ho rang du rango. Juba! Juba o, ye juba!" the crowd roared back.

Then came the Johnkankus leader himself. He was preceded by the gumbo box players, two dozen men strong. The gumbo box was a simple box covered with sheepskin. The singers set the rhymes, but the Johnkankus was dominated, created, by the beat of the gumbo box. *Boom, bam,* stomp, step, kick — Irene Jennie's feet paced sprightfully to the Johnkankus beat.

"Beat dat box again!" the crowd shouted. And the gumbo box beat, beat, beat. Heaven itself must have heard those Koners beating. Almost as loud as the gumbo boxes, matching them beat for beat, were the sounds of the triangles, jawbones, and beef ribs played by the other musicians. Masks askew, they beat at the sky, colors flying. Irene Jennie beat the sides of her thighs, making her own gumbo box.

This year the Johnkankus leader was a mountain of a man, nigh 'bout seven feet tall. With a stuffed animal skin for a hat, he towered at eight feet. "That man so tall, he mosn't scrape the clouds out the sky," Irene Jennie exclaimed in wonder. The Johnkankus was dressed in an old robe, red and green trimmed with what looked like fur. On his fingers were ribbons attached to bells, and his arms were filled with metal bracelets and arm rings that chimed as he danced. About his shoulders were strings of dried goat's horns.

Irene Jennie squealed with laughter. "Godmama, you see that?" she asked.

"I see it, chile," the Godmother said as she did a few Koner steps herself. Irene Jennie grabbed her hand, and they danced together just as the Johnkankus danced. First he jigged and then he jiggled back. Next he hunched his back, then straightened it out, kicking and flinging his legs up high. The Johnkankus caroused in the air. As he danced, two acrobats did back flips, one on each side of him. The slave quarter went wild.

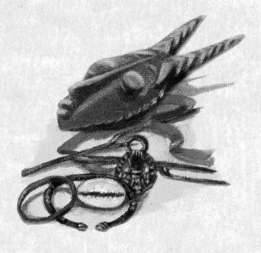

Suddenly there was a moment of silence as the Johnkankus started his special dance, showing his best steps and movements, dancing where the spirit moved him. Ringed around him were his court: the beast men, the bird men, the musicians, the acrobats, and the dancers. Irene Jennie looked on in amazement. The Johnkankus finished, and the crowd erupted.

As the melee and movement died down, the handsomest of the Koners, dressed in his church clothes and carrying a tin cup, went to each person and sang out for a dram of rum or a penny or two.

Oh poor Koner Johns,
For me, for me, my lady,
Give the poor Koners one more cent,
For me, for me, my lady.

The Godmother pressed one shiny penny into Irene Jennie's hand, and Irene Jennie dropped it into the cup, saying, "Thankee."

Toward dusk the line of Koners marched on, heading toward the big house, singing and dancing Christmas Day away. As the excitement in the quarters died down, Irene Jennie started to remember how much she missed her mama and daddy. Her laughter waned to smiles; her smiles were weakening into tears. "Lord, all I wants for Christmas is my mama and daddy back," she whispered. She downheartedly watched the last of the Koner line. Suddenly Irene Jennie couldn't believe what she was hearing. She couldn't believe what she was seeing.

There was her daddy, fiddling, and her mama, dancing, at the end of the parade.

"Jubilee!" she shouted. "Jubilee, jubilee! Mama, mama, daddy, daddy!"

Irene Jennie ran and, in her eagerness, jumped first on her mother and then on her father. "How's Mama's sweet baby girl doing?" Mary Ellen asked.

Irene Jennie's daddy continued: "You know, it was the strangest thing. We had a whole mess of cleaning up to do after the party, but Massa allus sudden told us to head home. He didn't have to tell us twice."

Mary Ellen finished with "We knew you'd be missin' us. And it's never too late to celebrate Christmas."

Together they said, "Merry Christmas, Irene Jennie."

"I'se fixin' to bust with happiness," Irene Jennie blurted out. She smiled the biggest grin and said a silent *Thank you, Lord.*

From the side of the road, the Godmother shouted, "Hallelujah! Y'all have one merry Christmas, now." Then she turned and headed for her cabin.

As Irene Jennie and her family kissed and hugged, the Koners' chorusing and music could still clearly be heard from up at the big house.

Poor Massa, so dey say,
Down in the heel, so dey say,
Got no money, so dey say,
Not one shilling, so dey say,
God a-mighty bress you, so dey say.

Between hugs and kisses, Irene Jennie said, "The Koners' laughter and shouts sho' makes a perfect Christmas serenade. And to make things even better, my Christmas prayer been answered. I has the bestest Christmas present of all. This time I'se got my mama and daddy back."

Hah, low, here we go,
Hah, low, here we go,
Koners going!
Hah, low, here we go,
Koners going!

The Johnkankus troupe was on its way to the next plantation. "Hah, low, here we go," Irene Jennie chorused. *This surely is one great Christmas Day,* she thought as she tapped her foot to the *beat beat beat* of the gumbo box.